PUFFIN BOOKS

OLD TOM'S

Guide to Being Good

Written and Illustrated by

Leigh HOBBS

For Erica Irving & Dmetri Kakmi

Puffin Books
Penguin Books Australia Ltd
487 Maroondah Highway, PO Box 257
Ringwood, Victoria 3134, Australia
Penguin Books Ltd
Harmondsworth, Middlesex, England
Penguin Putnam Inc.
375 Hudson Street, New York, New York 10014, USA
Penguin Books Canada Limited
10 Alcorn Avenue, Toronto, Ontario, Canada M4V 3B2
Penguin Books (N.Z.) Ltd
Cnr Rosedale and Airborne Roads, Albany, Auckland New Zealand
Penguin Books South Africa Pty Ltd
4 Palinghurst Road, Parktown 2193, South Africa

First published by Penguin Books Australia, 1998
1 3 5 7 9 10 8 6 4 2
Copyright © Leigh Hobbs, 1998
Illustrations Copyright © Leigh Hobbs, 1998

Desktopped and designed by Marina Messiha, Penguin Design Studio
Made and printed in Australia by Australian Print Group,
Maryborough, Victoria

National Library of Australia
Cataloguing-in-Publication data:

Hobbs, Leigh.
Old Tom's guide to being good.
ISBN 0 14 038590 8.
1. Title.
A823.3

'I'm tired of the same old faces at my garden parties,' said the Queen with a sigh.

'Why not pick a name from the telephone book, Your Majesty?' suggested Sir Tassel Windburn, her able secretary.

'Splendid,' said the Queen.
Soon the royal finger stopped at a surname
beginning with 'T'.

And so, when Old Tom went to collect the
mail one day,

there was a fancy looking letter, for Angela
Throgmorton.

She was enjoying a well-earned rest, having
cleaned the house from top to bottom.

But this was a letter that couldn't wait.
A royal invitation for two, for afternoon tea.

Angela knew the Queen was fussy about
good manners. So she dressed up and
wrote back straight away.

Angela had done her best to bring Old
Tom up nicely.

He often happily helped around the house,

and sometimes did two chores at once.

But now that he was to meet the Queen,

Old Tom needed extra instruction in
how to be good.

Angela invited a friend for tea.
'Pretend it's the Queen and practise your
manners,' she said.

Old Tom had learnt from his lessons that a nice smile is always handy.

He was eager to please and keen to be good.

So, when Angela's guest felt a little unwell,
kind Old Tom kept an eye on her.

Meanwhile, Angela went on with her eating
instructions. 'If offered cake,' she said, 'say
yes, please, and thank you, and don't drop
your crumbs.'

There was a lot to remember, but Old Tom
was pleased with his progress.

Though Angela felt there was still work to be done.

In fact, Angela was desperate.

But time had run out and Old Tom was as
good as he was going to get.

So Angela and Old Tom packed their bags
and off they went.

Angela was excited . . .

. . . and so was Old Tom.

After his journey, Old Tom was tired.

PASSPORTS

'I've never seen anything like this before,'
said the passport man.

At the hotel,

Angela explained that she was on a royal visit.

Then, in the evening, Old Tom and Angela
practised their curtsies and bows.

Angela put on some gloves and pretended to be the Queen.

'Kiss my hand,' she said.

In the morning, Angela got up bright and
early. Old Tom had to have a bath …

... and she was needed to remove difficult oily patches.

This was a big day, and Old Tom planned
to look especially beautiful.

So, all morning, he combed and brushed
and fussed and even had his nails done.

When the arrival of lunch stopped him
cleaning his teeth,

he still remembered his manners, and gave
a big smile.

Luckily, Old Tom's good looks hadn't gone to his head.

Angela, too, had spent hours getting ready.
Now it was time for afternoon tea.

So Old Tom and Angela caught a bus to
the palace.

When they arrived, Angela whispered,
'Now, remember your lessons and you'll
blend in quite nicely.'

Angela had expected only three for tea.
But she was polite and hid her disappointment.

Old Tom was on his best behaviour,

while Angela began to introduce herself
and make polite conversation.

'Angela Throgmorton's my name,' she said,
'and I'm here to meet the Queen.'

'Aren't we all?' replied Sir Cecil Snootypants.

At first, Old Tom was a little shy.

But soon he relaxed and made himself comfortable.

Angela kept an eye on things and whispered
helpful hints when no one was looking.

Old Tom remembered to look people
straight in the eye and make them feel special.

Then he had a rest from being good and
made himself a sandwich.

Being good had certainly improved
his appetite.

Old Tom made friends quickly and even
found a favourite.

He was careful, of course, to leave room
for dessert.

Meanwhile, Angela was having a lovely time.

'What an unusual hat!' mumbled Boswell Croswell.

'I'm glad you like it,' was her gracious reply.

The afternoon-tea party was now in
full swing.

'I hear the Queen has been delayed,'
said Lady Arabella Volcano to her
husband Horace.

While chatting to Sir Basil Bossy and his
charming wife Babette, Angela noticed
that Old Tom had gone.

She excused herself and began to search.
Angela tried to tempt Old Tom out with a
fresh chicken leg.

Angela described Old Tom to everyone she met.

'Oh, my goodness!' cried Sir Bertie Boodle.

'Good gracious!' shrieked Lady Winifred
Pineapple De Groote and her husband
Sir Ernest.

He has one eye, pointy ears and a hairy face.

'It can't be human!' cried Clarissa Cul-de-Sac just before she fainted.

Angela had mislaid
Old Tom, and wanted
him back before the
royal host arrived.

'By the way, where *is* the Queen?' asked Sir
Dalvin Dooper.

Suddenly there was silence, apart from a
tiny shriek from Lady Pineapple.

Her Majesty had arrived at last ...

. . . and she had company.

Angela was thrilled to see Old Tom and
nearly forgot her manners.

But not for long, of course.

'So you are my *other* special guest! I've
already met Old Tom,' said the Queen.
'And what jolly fun we've had!'

Her Majesty insisted that they stay the night.

After dinner there was a royal tour.
'That's my throne,' said the Queen.
And then it was time for bed.

Hot
Chocolate
for
Sir?

The comfort of her guests was most
important. So that . . .

... at breakfast, even if the Queen *had* seen
Old Tom's little mistake, she was too polite
to comment.

Goodbye!

Soon it was time to say goodbye.
The Queen had her royal duties and
Angela had work to do around the house.

As for Old Tom, he was happy with a kiss
from Angela, his guide to being good.

ABOUT THE AUTHOR

Leigh Hobbs was born in Melbourne in 1953, but grew up in a country town called Bairnsdale. His first job as an artist was at Sydney's Luna Park where he supervised the restoration of a carousel and created two huge caricature figures called Larry and Lizzy Luna. He has illustrated numerous children's books and many of his cartoons have appeared in the Melbourne *Age* newspaper.

Leigh has a passion for English history. His favourite place is London, where he lived for a while and which he visits regularly.

Read these books and join Old Tom
on all his adventures.

Old Tom
Old Tom at the Beach
Old Tom goes to Mars